mysterious journey

THRU THE STREETS OF KOLKATA

AVISHEK TRIVEDI

BLUEROSE PUBLISHERS
India | U.K.

Copyright © Avishek Trivedi 2024

All rights reserved by author. No part of this publication may be reproduced, stored in a retrieval system or transmitted in any form or by any means, electronic, mechanical, photocopying, recording or otherwise, without the prior permission of the author. Although every precaution has been taken to verify the accuracy of the information contained herein, the publisher assumes no responsibility for any errors or omissions. No liability is assumed for damages that may result from the use of information contained within.

BlueRose Publishers takes no responsibility for any damages, losses, or liabilities that may arise from the use or misuse of the information, products, or services provided in this publication.

For permissions requests or inquiries regarding this publication,
please contact:

BLUEROSE PUBLISHERS
www.BlueRoseONE.com
info@bluerosepublishers.com
+91 8882 898 898
+4407342408967

ISBN: 978-93-6452-282-3

Cover design: Shivam
Typesetting: Namrata Saini

First Edition: Ocotber 2024

Preface

In the swirling vortex of India's vibrant cities, lies a hidden world of ancient secrets, mysterious energies, and untold stories. Kolkata, the City of Joy, stands as a testament to this enigmatic landscape, where the past and present converge in a kaleidoscope of color, sound, and emotion.

This novel is a journey into the heart of Kolkata, where Raju, stumble upon a hidden reality that threatens to upend their lives forever. As he navigate the city's hidden corners, crumbling architecture, and whispered legends, he discover that the line between reality and myth blurs.

Inspired by the city's rich cultural heritage and the resilience of its people, this story explores the universal themes of friendship, self-discovery, and the struggle between light and darkness.

Through the eyes of Raju, we experience the pulsing rhythm of Kolkata, its contradictions and paradoxes, and the transformative power of determination.

Join me on this captivating journey into the soul of Kolkata, where secrets await, mysteries unfold, and the boundaries of reality are tested.

Introduction

"In the sweltering heat of Kolkata, where the ancient and modern worlds collide, a young man named Raju stumbles upon a mysterious diary that sets him on a perilous journey to uncover the secrets of the city. As he delves deeper into the heart of Kolkata, he discovers a hidden world of ancient treasures, cursed riches, and forgotten histories. But Raju soon realizes that he is not alone in his quest, and that the truth he seeks is guarded by powerful forces that will stop at nothing to keep it hidden. Will Raju be able to unravel the mysteries of Kolkata before it's too late, or will the city's secrets consume him forever?"

Contents

Chapter 1: The Streets of Kolkata 1

Chapter 2: The Ganges River 3

Chapter 3: The Shadow in the Alley 5

Chapter 4: The Mysterious Ally 8

Chapter 5: The Hidden World 10

Chapter 6: The Unexpected Visitor 12

Chapter 7: The Web of Deceit 15

Chapter 8: The Trail of Clues 18

Chapter 9: The Darkness Closes In 22

Chapter 10: Into the Lion's Den 28

Chapter 11: Reverberations 32

Chapter 12: The Rescue 36

Chapter 13: The Warehouse 41

Chapter 14: The Betrayal 45

Chapter 15: The Unexpected Ally 48

Chapter 16: The Enigmatic Stranger 51

Chapter 17: The Hidden Agenda 54

Chapter 18: The Pursuit 56

Chapter 19: Back to the Streets 58

Chapter 20: The Red Vipers 60

Chapter 21: The Aftermath 62

Chapter 22: The Hidden Truth 64

Chapter 23: The Dark Alleys of Kolkata 66

Chapter 24: The Lost Friend 68

Chapter 25: The Watchers 70

Chapter 26: The Disappearance 72

Chapter 27: The City of Secrets 75

Chapter 28: The Tunnel Network 78

Chapter 29: The Hidden Chamber 80

Chapter 30: The Awakening 83

Chapter 31: The Midnight Meeting 85

Epilogue 87

Acknowledgements 88

Disclaimer 89

CHAPTER 1

The Streets of Kolkata

The sun had barely risen over the bustling streets of Kolkata, but already the city was alive with activity. Cars honked, vendors shouted, and the smell of street food wafted through the air.

In the midst of this chaos, a young boy named Raju navigated the crowded sidewalks with ease. His dark eyes darted back and forth, scanning the pavement for scraps to eat or coins to collect.

Raju was just twelve years old, but he had been living on the streets for as long as he could remember. His mother had died when he was just a baby, and his father had abandoned him soon after.

With no family to care for him, Raju had learned to rely on his wits and his cunning to survive. He was small and quick, able to dodge through the crowds with ease.

As he walked, Raju's stomach growled with hunger. He hadn't eaten since the previous day, and he knew he needed to find something soon.

He spotted a vendor selling fresh fruit and made a beeline for the cart. The vendor, a kind-eyed old man, saw Raju approaching and smiled.

"Hey, little one," he said, offering Raju a juicy orange. "Eat this, and don't worry about paying me back."

Raju's eyes lit up as he took the orange and devoured it in mere moments. The sweet juice ran down his chin, and he wiped it away with the back of his hand.

"Thank you, uncle," he said, grinning.

The vendor smiled and ruffled Raju's hair. "Be careful out there, okay?"

Raju nodded and continued on his way, his eyes scanning the streets for the next opportunity.

But little did he know, his life was about to take a dramatic turn.

CHAPTER 2

The Ganges River

Raju continued his journey through the winding streets of Kolkata, his eyes fixed on the pavement beneath his feet. He knew every alleyway, every corner, and every vendor by name.

As he walked, the sounds of the city grew louder, and the smell of incense and spices filled the air. Raju's stomach growled once more, reminding him that he needed to find more food.

He made his way towards the Ganges River, where he knew he could find scraps to eat and possibly even some work. The river was the lifeblood of Kolkata, and Raju had grown up playing on its banks.

As he approached the river, Raju saw a group of children his age, washing clothes in the murky water. He recognized some of them from his own neighborhood and waved in greeting.

One of the children, a girl named Leela, caught his eye. She was a year older than Raju, with piercing green eyes and long, dark hair. She smiled at him, and Raju felt a flutter in his chest. "Raju, come help us!" Leela called out, gesturing to the pile of clothes beside her.

Raju hesitated for a moment before joining the group. Together, they washed and rinsed the clothes, laughing and joking as they worked.

As they finished up, Leela turned to Raju with a serious expression. "Be careful, Raju," she said. "There's talk of a new gang in town, looking for kids like us to join their ranks."

Raju's heart skipped a beat. He had heard rumors of gangs before, but he never thought they would come looking for him.

"Don't worry, Leela," he said, trying to sound braver than he felt. "I can take care of myself."

Leela nodded, but her eyes betrayed her concern.

As Raju walked away from the river, he couldn't shake the feeling that his life was about to change forever.

CHAPTER 3

The Shadow in the Alley

Raju navigated the narrow alleys of Kolkata, his senses on high alert. He had been warned about the new gang, and he knew he needed to be careful.

As he turned a corner, he noticed a figure lurking in the shadows. The figure was tall and imposing, with a scar above his left eyebrow.

Raju's heart raced as the figure stepped forward, its eyes fixed on him. "You're the one they call Raju, aren't you?" it said, its voice low and menacing.

Raju nodded, trying to hide his fear. "Who are you?" he demanded.

The figure smiled, revealing crooked teeth. "My name is Kala, and I'm here to offer you a deal."

Raju hesitated, unsure of what to do. But Kala's words were laced with a hint of promise, and Raju's curiosity got the better of him.

"What kind of deal?" he asked, his voice barely above a whisper. Kala leaned in, his breath hot against Raju's ear. "Join us, and you'll never have to scrounge for food or shelter again. You'll be part of something big, something powerful."

Raju's mind reeled as Kala's words painted a picture of a life he had never known. A life of security, of belonging.

But something didn't feel right. Raju's instincts screamed at him to run, to get as far away from Kala as possible.

"I don't know," he said, trying to stall.

Kala's smile grew wider. "Oh, I think you do," he said, his eyes glinting with a sinister light. "You see, Raju, we've been watching you. We know all about your little tricks, your survival skills. You'd be a valuable asset to our team."

Raju knew he had to make a decision. Join Kala's gang, or risk everything to stay on his own.

Raju hesitated, weighing his options. He had always been on his own, relying on his wits to survive. But Kala's words echoed in his mind, tempting him with promises of security and belonging.

Just as he was about to make a decision, a loud noise echoed through the alley, making them both jump. Kala's eyes narrowed, and he grabbed Raju's arm, pulling him deeper into the shadows.

"What was that?" Raju whispered, his heart racing.

Kala's grip tightened. "Just a stray animal," he hissed. "But we need to get out of here, now."

Raju tried to shake off Kala's grip, but it only tightened. He was trapped.

Suddenly, a figure emerged from the darkness, its eyes fixed on Kala. "Let him go," it growled.

Kala sneered, but Raju saw a flicker of fear in his eyes. "Mind your own business," Kala snarled.

The figure took a step closer, its eyes blazing with intensity. "He's not one of yours," it said. "Leave him alone."

Raju's heart pounded as Kala's grip finally relaxed. He took advantage of the distraction to wriggle free, backing away from Kala and the mysterious figure.

"Who are you?" Raju demanded, trying to keep his voice steady.

The figure turned to him, its eyes softening. "My name is Amit," it said. "And I'm here to help you."

Raju's mind reeled as Amit's words hung in the air. Could he trust this stranger? Or was Amit just another predator, waiting to pounce?

CHAPTER 4

The Mysterious Ally

Raju's eyes narrowed, unsure of what to make of Amit's sudden appearance. But there was something in Amit's eyes that put him at ease - a deep kindness and concern.

"What do you want from me?" Raju asked, trying to sound cautious.

Amit smiled, his eyes crinkling at the corners. "I want to help you, Raju. I've been watching you from afar, and I know you're in danger. Kala's gang is not to be trusted."

Raju's instincts screamed at him to run, but Amit's words struck a chord. He had been feeling like he was in over his head, like the streets were getting more and more treacherous.

"Why would you help me?" Raju asked, his voice barely above a whisper.

Amit's expression turned serious. "Because I know what it's like to be alone on the streets. I know what it's like to have no one to turn to. But I also know that there's a better life out there, Raju. And I want to help you find it."

Raju's heart swelled with emotion as Amit's words resonated deep within him. No one had ever offered to help him before, at least not without wanting something in return.

"Come with me," Amit said, holding out his hand.

Raju hesitated for a moment before taking it. As they walked away from the alley, Raju felt a sense of hope that he hadn't felt in years.

But little did he know, Kala's gang was watching from the shadows, their eyes fixed on Raju with a sinister intent.

CHAPTER 5

The Hidden World

Raju followed Amit through the winding streets of Kolkata, his senses on high alert. They navigated through crowded markets and narrow alleys, eventually arriving at a nondescript door hidden behind a tattered curtain.

Amit produced a small key and unlocked the door, revealing a dimly lit stairway that descended into darkness. "Welcome to my home," he said, gesturing for Raju to follow.

Raju hesitated, unsure of what lay ahead. But Amit's kind eyes reassured him, and he began to make his way down the stairs.

At the bottom, Raju found himself in a cozy, cramped room filled with books, strange artifacts, and a small kitchenette. Amit smiled, seeing his wonder. "This is my sanctuary," he said. "Few people know it exists."

Raju's eyes widened as Amit began to prepare a simple meal. He had never seen so much food in one place before.

As they ate, Amit told Raju about his own life on the streets, about the struggles and the dangers. But he also spoke of hope and resilience, of the power of the human spirit.

Raju listened, entranced, feeling like he had found a long-lost brother.

But as the night wore on, Raju began to realize that Amit was hiding something. He seemed to be waiting for something, or someone.

And then, just as Raju was starting to feel at ease, a knock at the door made them both jump.

Amit's eyes locked onto Raju's, filled with a warning. "Don't move," he whispered, before disappearing up the stairs.

Raju's heart pounded as he waited, his senses on high alert. Who was at the door? And what did they want?

CHAPTER 6

The Unexpected Visitor

Raju waited with bated breath as Amit disappeared up the stairs. He heard muffled voices, a low conversation that seemed to be growing more heated by the second.

Suddenly, Amit reappeared, his face tense. "Raju, I need to ask you something," he said, his voice low and urgent. "Can I trust you?"

Raju nodded, unsure of what was happening. "Of course, Amit. What's going on?"

Amit hesitated before answering. "The person at the door... it's someone from my past. Someone I thought I'd never see again."

Raju's curiosity was piqued. "Who is it?" he asked, his voice barely above a whisper.

Amit took a deep breath before answering. "It's my brother, Rohan. We were separated years ago, and I thought he was dead."

Raju's eyes widened in shock. "What does he want?" he asked, his mind racing with possibilities.

Amit's expression turned grim. "I don't know, but I need to find out. Stay here, Raju. I'll handle this."

Raju nodded, feeling a sense of trepidation. Who was Rohan, and what did he want with Amit?

As Amit disappeared up the stairs once more, Raju couldn't shake the feeling that their lives were about to change forever.

Raju waited anxiously as Amit disappeared up the stairs. He heard muffled voices, a low conversation that seemed to be growing more heated by the second.

As the minutes ticked by, Raju's curiosity grew. Who was Rohan, and what did he want with Amit? And why did Amit seem so wary of him?

Finally, the voices ceased, and Amit reappeared, his face tense. "Raju, I need to tell you something," he said, his voice low and urgent. "My brother, Rohan... he's not what he seems."

Raju's eyes narrowed. "What do you mean?" he asked, his voice barely above a whisper.

Amit hesitated before answering. "Rohan was always trouble, even as a child. He got involved with some bad people, and... and I thought he was dead."

Raju's eyes widened in shock. "But he's not," he stated, his mind racing with possibilities.

Amit shook his head. "No, he's not. And now he's here, asking for my help."

Raju's curiosity was piqued. "What kind of help?" he asked, his voice full of wonder.

Amit's expression turned grim. "I don't know, but I'm not going to give it to him. I have a feeling he's involved in something big, something dangerous."

Raju's heart pounded as he realized the implications. Amit was in danger, and he needed Raju's help to stay safe.

CHAPTER 7

The Web of Deceit

Raju's mind raced as he tried to process the information. Amit's brother, Rohan, was involved in something dangerous, and Amit was in grave danger.

"Amit, what are we going to do?" Raju asked, his voice laced with concern.

Amit's expression turned determined. "We need to get out of here, Raju. Now."

Raju nodded, and together they gathered their belongings and slipped out into the night. They navigated the crowded streets, avoiding detection by Rohan's associates.

As they walked, Amit told Raju more about his past, about the struggles he had faced growing up on the streets. Raju listened, entranced, feeling a deep connection to this man who had taken him under his wing.

But despite the danger, Raju couldn't shake the feeling that Amit was hiding something from him. Something big.

"Amit, can I ask you something?" Raju said, his voice barely above a whisper.
Amit nodded, his eyes scanning the crowds. "What is it, Raju?"

Raju hesitated before speaking. "What's really going on, Amit? What's Rohan involved in?"

Amit's expression turned grim, and for a moment, Raju thought he saw a flicker of fear in his eyes.

"I'll tell you everything, Raju," Amit promised. "But first, we need to get to a safe place."

Raju nodded, and together they continued on their journey, navigating the treacherous streets of Kolkata.

As they walked, Raju noticed that Amit seemed to know the streets intimately, navigating the crowded alleys with ease. They eventually arrived at a small, nondescript building, where Amit produced a key and unlocked the door.

Inside, the room was sparse, with only a few pieces of furniture. But what caught Raju's attention was the collection of books and papers scattered across the floor.

"Amit, what is all this?" Raju asked, his curiosity piqued.

Amit smiled, his eyes lighting up. "This is my research, Raju. I've been investigating Rohan's activities for months."

Raju's eyes widened as he began to understand. "You're trying to take him down," he said, his voice full of admiration.

Amit nodded, his expression grim. "I am. But it's not going to be easy. Rohan has connections, powerful ones. We need to be careful."

Raju nodded, feeling a sense of determination. He was in this now, and he was going to help Amit bring Rohan down.

As they began to sift through the papers, Raju realized that Amit's research was extensive. There were documents, photographs, and notes, all detailing Rohan's involvement in a massive human trafficking ring.

Raju's heart pounded as he read through the documents, his mind reeling with the implications. This was big, really big. And Amit was right in the middle of it.

CHAPTER 8

The Trail of Clues

Raju's eyes scanned the documents, his mind racing with the implications. Amit's research was meticulous, detailing a vast network of traffickers and corrupt officials.

"Amit, this is incredible," Raju said, his voice full of admiration. "You're a genius."

Amit smiled, his eyes tired. "I've had a lot of help, Raju. But we're not done yet. We need to follow the trail of clues."

Raju nodded, his heart pounding with excitement. He was in this now, and he was going to see it through.

Together, they pored over the documents, following a trail of cryptic messages and hidden codes. It was like a puzzle, and Raju was determined to solve it.

As they worked, Raju noticed that Amit seemed to be hiding something. He would glance at a document, then quickly look away, his expression guarded.

"Amit, what's going on?" Raju asked, his voice low. "You're hiding something from me."

Amit hesitated, then nodded. "I am, Raju. But I promise you, it's for your own protection."

Raju's eyes narrowed. "Tell me," he demanded.

Amit sighed, his expression resigned. "Rohan is just a small part of this, Raju. There's someone else, someone powerful, pulling the strings."

Raju's heart skipped a beat. "Who?" he asked, his voice barely above a whisper.

Amit's eyes locked onto Raju's, his expression grim. "I don't know yet, but I'm going to find out."

Raju's mind reeled as he tried to process the information. Someone powerful was behind the trafficking ring, and Amit was determined to find out who.

"What's the next step?" Raju asked, his voice firm.

Amit nodded, a plan forming in his eyes. "We need to follow the money trail. See where it leads us."

Raju nodded, his heart pounding with excitement. He was in this now, and he was going to see it through.

Together, they pored over financial records, following a trail of transactions that led them deeper into the heart of the trafficking ring.

As they worked, Raju noticed that Amit seemed to be getting more and more agitated. His eyes would flash with anger, and his hands would clench into fists.

"Amit, what's wrong?" Raju asked, his voice soft.

Amit's expression turned grim. "I know one of the victims, Raju. A girl named Sophia. She was like a sister to me."

Raju's heart went out to Amit. He could see the pain in his eyes, the determination to bring down those responsible.

"We'll find them, Amit," Raju promised. "We'll bring them down."

Amit nodded, his eyes locked onto Raju's. "Together, we will."

As they delved deeper into the financial records, they discovered a web of shell companies and secret accounts. But Amit's sharp mind was able to unravel the threads, leading them closer to the truth.

Suddenly, Amit's eyes widened as he stared at a particular transaction. "Raju, look at this," he whispered urgently.

Raju leaned in, his heart racing. The transaction was a large payment to a company called "Kolkata Enterprises".

"What is it?" Raju asked, his voice barely above a whisper.

Amit's expression turned grim. "That's the company owned by the Chief Minister's son."

Raju's eyes widened in shock. They had stumbled into something big, something that went all the way to the top.

"We need to be careful," Amit warned. "We're playing with fire now."

Raju nodded, his mind racing with the implications. They had to tread carefully, or they would be silenced forever.

As they continued to dig, they uncovered more evidence of corruption and deceit. But with each new discovery, they knew they were getting closer to the truth.

And closer to danger.

CHAPTER 9

The Darkness Closes In

Raju and Amit knew they had to move fast. They had uncovered a web of corruption that went all the way to the top, and they knew they were running out of time.

As they walked through the crowded streets of Kolkata, Raju couldn't shake the feeling that they were being watched. He glanced over his shoulder, but saw nothing.

"Amit, I think we're being followed," Raju whispered urgently.

Amit's eyes scanned the crowds, his expression grim. "Keep walking," he said. "Don't look back."

They quickened their pace, weaving through the throngs of people. But Raju could feel eyes upon him, boring into his skin.

Suddenly, Amit grabbed his arm and pulled him into a narrow alleyway. "In here," he whispered.

Raju followed, his heart pounding. They hid in the shadows, watching as a group of men walked by, their eyes scanning the crowds.

"They're looking for us," Amit whispered. "We need to get out of here, now."

Raju nodded, his mind racing. They knew too much, and now they were in grave danger.

As they emerged from the alleyway, Raju saw a figure waiting for them. It was Sophia, the girl Amit had told him about.

"Amit, thank God I found you," Sophia said, her eyes wide with fear. "They're closing in on us. We need to get out of Kolkata, now."

Amit nodded, his expression grim. "We'll get out, Sophia. I promise."

But as they turned to leave, Raju saw the men from the alleyway, their eyes fixed on them with a sinister intent.
Chapter 9: The Darkness Closes In (continued)

Raju's heart skipped a beat as the men began to close in on them. Amit grabbed his arm and Sophia's, pulling them into a nearby market.

They wove through the stalls, dodging vendors and customers. But the men were relentless, their footsteps echoing through the crowded market.

Amit spotted a small door hidden behind a stall. "In here," he whispered, pushing Raju and Sophia through the doorway.

They found themselves in a narrow, dimly lit corridor. Amit locked the door behind them, his chest heaving with exertion.

"We need to keep moving," he whispered. "They'll find us if we stay here."

Raju nodded, his mind racing. They were trapped, with no way out.

Sophia grabbed Amit's arm. "I know a way," she whispered. "Follow me."

She led them through the winding corridors, dodging shadows and hiding from the men who were closing in on them.

Finally, they emerged into a crowded street, the sounds of the city swallowing them whole.

But Raju knew they weren't safe yet. The men would find them, and next time, they wouldn't be so lucky.

They hailed a taxi and sped through the city, the men in pursuit. Raju glanced back, his heart racing with fear.

Sophia clutched Amit's arm, her eyes wide with terror. "Where are we going?" she whispered.

Amit's jaw was set, his eyes fixed on the road ahead. "Somewhere safe," he promised.

But Raju knew there was no such place. The men would find them, no matter where they hid.

The taxi screeched to a halt, and Amit pulled them out into a crowded market. They disappeared into the throngs of people, but Raju knew it was only a matter of time before they were found.

As they walked, Sophia stumbled, her eyes fixed on something ahead. Raju followed her gaze, his heart sinking.

The men had found them.

Amit grabbed their arms, pulling them into a nearby alleyway. But it was a dead end, with no escape.

The men closed in, their eyes cold and hard. Raju knew they were finished.

But then, a figure emerged from the shadows. A tall, imposing man with a fierce determination in his eyes.

"Leave them alone," he growled, his voice low and menacing.

The men hesitated, then backed away. The figure turned to Raju, Amit, and Sophia.

"Come with me," he said. "I'll keep you safe."

Raju hesitated, unsure of what to do. But Amit nodded, his eyes locked on the stranger.

"Trust him," he whispered.

And with that, they followed the stranger into the unknown.

The stranger led them through winding alleys and narrow streets, finally stopping at a nondescript door. He produced a key and unlocked it, revealing a dimly lit stairway.

"Down here," he said, gesturing for them to follow.

Raju hesitated, but Amit nodded, his eyes fixed on the stranger. They descended the stairs, finding themselves in a cramped, dimly lit room.

The stranger introduced himself as Ramesh, a former police officer turned vigilante. He had been tracking the trafficking ring for months, and knew Amit's research was the key to taking them down.

Raju's eyes widened as Ramesh revealed his plan. They would go undercover, gathering evidence from within the ring. It was dangerous, but Ramesh promised to keep them safe.

Amit nodded, his jaw set. "I'm in."

Sophia hesitated, fear in her eyes. But Raju knew they had no choice. They had to take down the ring, no matter the cost.

"I'm in too," Raju said, his voice firm.

Ramesh nodded, a small smile on his face. "Welcome to the team."

As they began to plan their undercover operation, Raju couldn't shake the feeling that they were walking into darkness. But he knew they had to try.

For the sake of the victims, they had to try.

CHAPTER 10

Into the Lion's Den

Raju, Amit, and Sophia stood outside the dilapidated building, their hearts racing with anticipation. This was it – their chance to infiltrate the trafficking ring and gather evidence.

Ramesh handed them each a small earpiece. "Stay in touch," he whispered. "I'll be monitoring from outside."

They nodded, took a deep breath, and stepped inside.

The air was thick with smoke and despair. Raju's eyes adjusted slowly, revealing a dimly lit room filled with people. Some were huddled in corners, others sat listlessly on the floor.

Amit nudged him forward. "Let's move," he whispered.

They wove through the crowd, trying to blend in. Sophia clutched Raju's arm, her eyes wide with fear.

A figure emerged from the shadows – Rohan, Amit's brother.

"Welcome, Amit," Rohan sneered. "I've been expecting you."

Amit's eyes locked onto Rohan, his jaw set. "I'm here to stop you," he said, his voice firm.

Rohan laughed. "You're too late for that. The operation is already in motion."

Raju's heart sank. They had to act fast.

Rohan snapped his fingers, and two burly men appeared, flanking Raju and Sophia. Amit stood tall, his eyes flashing with defiance.

"You're not going anywhere," Rohan sneered. "You're going to help me with the operation."

Amit spat at Rohan's feet. "I'll never help you."

Rohan's face twisted in rage. "Fine. You'll watch, then."

He gestured to a door at the far end of the room. Raju's heart sank as he realized what was about to happen.

The door creaked open, revealing a group of terrified girls, huddled together in fear. Raju recognized one of them - it was Maria, the girl he had met on the streets.

Rohan smiled. "The merchandise. And you, Amit, are going to help me sell it."

Amit's eyes locked onto Maria, his expression grim. Raju knew he had to act fast.

With a surge of adrenaline, Raju pushed forward, knocking aside the burly men. "Run!" he yelled to Sophia and the girls.

Chaos erupted as they made a break for the door. Raju fought off the men, his heart pounding in his chest.

They burst out into the night air, gasping for breath. Ramesh was waiting, his car screeching to a halt beside them.

"In!" he yelled. "Now!"

They piled in, speeding away from the scene. Raju glanced back, seeing Rohan's furious face in the distance.

They had escaped, but Raju knew it was only the beginning. The trafficking ring would stop at nothing to silence them.

Ramesh sped through the streets, his eyes fixed on the rearview mirror. "We need to get out of Kolkata," he said. "Now."

Amit nodded, his face grim. "We can't let them win."

Sophia clutched Raju's arm, her eyes wide with fear. "What about Maria?" she whispered.

Raju's heart ached. They had left Maria behind, trapped in the trafficking ring.

"We'll get her out," Raju promised. "I swear."

Ramesh's phone buzzed. He answered, listening intently. "It's done," he said, his voice tight. "The police are raiding the trafficking ring now."

Amit's eyes lit up with hope. "We did it," he whispered.

But Raju knew it wasn't over yet. The trafficking ring had tentacles everywhere, and they would fight back.

As they sped out of Kolkata, Raju gazed out at the city, his heart heavy with the knowledge of what they had faced.

But he also knew they had each other, and that together, they could overcome anything.

CHAPTER 11

Reverberations

Raju, Amit, Sophia, and Ramesh arrived at a safe house on the outskirts of Kolkata, exhausted but relieved. They had done it — they had taken down the trafficking ring.

But as they settled in, Raju couldn't shake the feeling of unease. Maria was still out there, trapped in the ring's clutches.

Ramesh noticed his concern. "We'll get her out, Raju. I promise."

Amit nodded. "We'll work with the police to rescue her."

Sophia smiled weakly. "We did it, guys. We made a difference."

But Raju knew it wasn't over yet. The trafficking ring's leaders were still at large, and they would stop at nothing to silence them.

As they rested, Raju's mind raced with thoughts of Maria and the others still trapped. He knew he had to do more.

Raju couldn't sleep, his mind racing with thoughts of Maria and the others. He knew he had to do more.

He got up, quietly making his way to Ramesh's room. "Ramesh, I need to talk to you," he whispered.

Ramesh opened his eyes, groggy. "What is it, Raju?"

"We can't just sit here," Raju said, his voice urgent. "We have to do something to help Maria and the others."

Ramesh sat up, rubbing his eyes. "I know, Raju. But we have to be smart. We can't just rush in without a plan."

Raju nodded, his mind racing. "I have an idea."

Ramesh raised an eyebrow. "What is it?"

Raju took a deep breath. "I'll go undercover, pretend to be a buyer. I can get inside and gather evidence, find out where Maria is."

Ramesh's eyes widened. "Raju, that's too dangerous."

But Raju was determined. "I have to do this, Ramesh. For Maria, for the others."

Ramesh sighed, knowing Raju's mind was made up. "Okay, let's do it. But we'll do it together, as a team."

Raju nodded, a plan forming in his mind.

Raju, Ramesh, Amit, and Sophia huddled together, planning their next move. They would go undercover, posing as buyers, to gather evidence and find Maria.

Ramesh handed Raju a small device. "This is a tracker," he explained. "It will help us keep tabs on you."

Raju nodded, his heart racing with anticipation.

Amit clapped him on the back. "Be careful, Raju. We'll be watching from outside."

Sophia's eyes were wide with worry. "Please, Raju, be safe."

Raju smiled, trying to reassure her. "I will, Sophia. I promise."

With a deep breath, Raju stepped out into the night, ready to face whatever lay ahead.

He made his way to the designated meeting point, a seedy bar on the outskirts of town. Raju's heart pounded as he entered, scanning the room for any sign of danger.

A figure emerged from the shadows, a sly smile spreading across his face. "Welcome, Raju. I've been expecting you."

Raju's instincts screamed warning, but he played it cool, pretending to be interested in the "merchandise".

As they negotiated, Raju's eyes scanned the room, searching for Maria. And then, he saw her, huddled in a corner, her eyes vacant.

Raju's heart skipped a beat. He had to get her out, now.

CHAPTER 12

The Rescue

Raju's eyes locked onto Maria, his heart racing with determination. He had to get her out, now.

He turned back to the trafficker, a smile plastered on his face. "I'll take her," he said, trying to sound convincing.

The trafficker sneered. "You'll pay top dollar for her."

Raju nodded, his mind racing. He had to stall for time, until Ramesh and the others could get into position.

As they negotiated, Raju subtly gestured to Maria, trying to signal to her that help was on the way.

Maria's eyes flickered, a glimmer of hope in their depths.

Raju's heart swelled with determination. He would save her, no matter what.

Just then, Ramesh burst into the room, followed by Amit and Sophia. "Police!" Ramesh yelled. "Everyone get down!"

The traffickers scrambled, trying to escape. Raju grabbed Maria's hand, pulling her to safety.

As they emerged into the night air, Maria's eyes locked onto Raju's, tears streaming down her face. "Thank you," she whispered.

Raju smiled, his heart full. "You're safe now," he said. "You're free."

The police closed in, arresting the traffickers. Raju watched, a sense of satisfaction washing over him.

They had done it. They had saved Maria.

But as they walked away from the scene, Raju knew it wasn't over yet. There were still others out there, trapped in the trafficking ring's clutches.

He turned to Ramesh, his eyes burning with determination. "We're not done yet," he said. "We have to save them all."

Ramesh nodded, a small smile on his face. "We will, Raju. Together."

Raju, Maria, Ramesh, Amit, and Sophia made their way back to the safe house, exhausted but triumphant. They had saved Maria, and they knew they could save others.

As they settled in, Maria began to open up, sharing her story of being trafficked and exploited. Raju listened, his heart heavy with emotion.

But as they talked, Raju realized that Maria's story was just the tip of the iceberg. There were countless others like her, trapped in the trafficking ring's clutches.

He knew they had to do more. They had to take down the trafficking ring once and for all.

Ramesh nodded in agreement. "We need to gather evidence, build a case against them."

Amit's eyes lit up. "I can help with that. I've been tracking their financial transactions."

Sophia smiled. "And I can help with the legal side. I've been studying trafficking laws."

Raju's heart swelled with pride. They were a team, united in their quest for justice.

Together, they began to gather evidence, building a case against the trafficking ring. It was a daunting task, but they were determined.

As they worked, Raju knew they were getting close. They were closing in on the traffickers.

But the traffickers wouldn't go down without a fight. Raju knew they would stop at nothing to silence them.

One night, as they were gathering evidence, Raju received a chilling message. "Back off, or you'll pay the price."

Raju knew it was from the traffickers. They were getting desperate.

But he refused to back down. He knew they were close to taking down the trafficking ring.

Ramesh, Amit, Sophia, and Maria stood by him, undaunted. "We're in this together," Ramesh said.

As they continued their work, the threats escalated. Raju received menacing calls, warning him to drop the case.

But he refused to give up. He knew they were making a difference.

And then, the unthinkable happened. Sophia was kidnapped by the traffickers.

Raju was devastated. He knew he had to act fast.

Ramesh, Amit, and Maria joined forces, racing against time to rescue Sophia.

They tracked the traffickers to an abandoned warehouse on the outskirts of town.

Raju's heart pounded as they approached the entrance. What would they find inside?

CHAPTER 13

The Warehouse

Raju's heart raced as they entered the warehouse, guns drawn. The air was thick with tension.

"Sophia!" Raju yelled, his voice echoing off the walls.

A faint noise came from the far corner. Raju sprinted towards it, Ramesh and Amit close behind.

As they turned a corner, Raju's blood ran cold. Sophia was tied to a chair, a gag over her mouth. But it was what was beside her that made Raju's heart stop.

A figure, shrouded in shadows, loomed over Sophia. Raju couldn't make out their features.

"Welcome, Raju," the figure said, their voice low and menacing. "I've been waiting for you."

Raju's eyes scanned the room, searching for any sign of danger. But there was nothing. Just the figure, Sophia, and an eerie silence.

"Who are you?" Raju demanded, trying to keep his voice steady. The figure stepped forward, revealing a shocking face. It was someone Raju knew, someone he trusted.

"You're one of us," Raju whispered, stunned.

The figure smiled, a cold, calculating smile. "I've been playing both sides all along."

Raju's mind reeled as the figure revealed their true intentions. He felt like he'd been punched in the gut.

And then, everything went black.

Raju's world went dark, his head spinning. When he came to, he was lying on the ground, his hands tied behind his back.

The figure stood over him, a smirk on their face. "You're so predictable, Raju."

Raju struggled against his bonds, but they were too tight. He was trapped.

The figure began to circle him, their eyes gleaming with malice. "You see, Raju, I've been playing a long game. And you're just a pawn."

Raju's mind raced, trying to understand. Who was this person? What did they want?

The figure leaned in, their voice dropping to a whisper. "I'm the one who's been controlling the trafficking ring all along."

Raju's eyes widened in shock. He couldn't believe it.

The figure straightened, a cold smile spreading across their face. "And now, Raju, you're going to help me take it to the next level."

Raju spat at their feet. "Never."

The figure laughed, a chilling sound. "Oh, I think you will. You see, I have something you want."

Raju's heart sank, knowing what was coming.

The figure gestured, and Sophia was dragged forward, a gun pressed to her head.

"Let her go!" Raju yelled, struggling against his bonds.

The figure smiled. "I don't think so. You see, Raju, you're going to do exactly what I say. Or Sophia dies."

Raju's world went dark, his heart heavy with despair.

Raju's eyes locked onto Sophia, his heart racing with fear. He knew he had to act fast.

"I'll do it," he said, his voice barely above a whisper.

The figure smiled, a triumphant glint in their eye. "I knew you'd see it my way."

Raju's mind raced, trying to think of a plan. He knew he couldn't trust this person, but he had to play along.

"What do you want me to do?" he asked, trying to keep his voice steady.

The figure leaned in, their voice dropping to a whisper. "I want you to help me take down Ramesh and Amit. They're getting too close to the truth."

Raju's heart sank, knowing he couldn't betray his friends. But he had to keep Sophia safe.

"Okay," he said, trying to sound convincing. "I'll do it."

The figure smiled, a cold, calculating smile. "Good. I knew I could count on you."

Raju's eyes locked onto Sophia, trying to convey a message. He knew he had to find a way to save her, and take down the figure.

But for now, he had to play along.

CHAPTER 14

The Betrayal

Raju's heart heavy with deceit, he pretended to cooperate with the figure. But secretly, he was plotting his next move.

He knew he had to protect Sophia and take down the figure. But how?

As they left the warehouse, Raju caught a glimpse of Ramesh and Amit watching from the shadows. He knew they were onto something.

The figure handed Raju a phone. "Call Ramesh. Tell him to meet you at the old clock tower at midnight. Alone."

Raju's mind raced. This was a trap.

But he had to play along. For Sophia's sake.

He dialed the number, his heart pounding in his chest.

"Ramesh, it's me. Meet me at the old clock tower at midnight. Alone."

Ramesh's voice was cautious. "What's going on, Raju?"

Raju hesitated, unsure how much to reveal. "Just trust me, Ramesh. Please."

Ramesh's silence was unsettling. But finally, he agreed. "Okay, Raju. I'll be there."

Raju hung up, his heart heavy with foreboding.

What was he getting himself into?

At midnight, Raju made his way to the old clock tower, his heart racing with anticipation. Sophia was by his side, her eyes fixed on him with a mix of fear and trust.

As they approached the tower, Ramesh emerged from the shadows. "Raju, what's going on?" he asked, his voice low and cautious.

Raju hesitated, unsure how much to reveal. But before he could speak, the figure emerged from the darkness.

"Welcome, Ramesh," they said, a sly smile spreading across their face. "I've been waiting for you."

Ramesh's eyes narrowed. "Who are you?"

The figure laughed. "Someone who's been playing you all along."

Raju's heart sank, knowing he had to act fast. But before he could move, the figure pulled out a gun.

"Raju, take care of your friend," they said, their voice cold and calculating.

Raju's eyes locked onto Ramesh, his heart heavy with regret. He knew he had to make a choice.

CHAPTER 15

The Unexpected Ally

Raju's eyes locked onto Ramesh, his heart heavy with regret. He knew he had to make a choice.

But just as he was about to act, Sophia broke free from her captor and tackled the figure to the ground.

The gun went flying, and Ramesh took advantage of the distraction to disarm the figure.

Raju's eyes widened in shock as Sophia stood up, a fierce look in her eyes.

"I'm not just a victim," she said, her voice firm. "I'm a survivor."

The figure struggled to their feet, revealing a shocking identity.

It was Amit, Raju's friend and ally.

Raju's world turned upside down. "Amit, why?" he asked, his voice shaking with betrayal.

Amit sneered. "You were always so blind, Raju. I've been playing you from the beginning."

But before Amit could reveal more, Sophia spoke up.

"I don't think so, Amit," she said, a sly smile spreading across her face. "You see, I've been playing you too."

Raju's eyes widened in shock as Sophia revealed her true identity.

She was the mastermind behind the trafficking ring.

Chapter 15: The Unexpected Ally (continued)

Raju's mind reeled as Sophia revealed her true identity. He couldn't believe he had trusted her.

But before he could react, Sophia dropped another bombshell.

"I've been working with Ramesh all along," she said, a sly smile spreading across her face.

Ramesh nodded, a hint of a smile on his face. "We've been playing a long game, Raju. Taking down the trafficking ring from the inside."

Raju's eyes widened in shock. He couldn't believe his friends had been deceiving him.

But as he looked at Sophia and Ramesh, he saw something unexpected - a glimmer of hope.

Maybe, just maybe, they could still take down the trafficking ring together.

"Amit, you're finished," Sophia said, her voice cold and calculating.

Amit snarled, but Raju could see the fear in his eyes.

And then, everything went black.

CHAPTER 16

The Enigmatic Stranger

Raju's eyes fluttered open, his head pounding with pain. He was lying in a dimly lit room, with no sign of Sophia, Ramesh, or Amit.

Suddenly, a figure emerged from the shadows. Tall, imposing, with piercing green eyes.

"Who are you?" Raju asked, trying to sit up.

The stranger didn't respond. Instead, they handed Raju a folder full of documents.

As Raju flipped through the pages, his eyes widened in shock. The documents revealed a web of corruption and deceit that went far beyond the trafficking ring.

"This is huge," Raju whispered.

The stranger nodded. "It's just the tip of the iceberg."

Raju looked up, trying to read the stranger's expression. But their face was a mask of mystery.

"Who are you?" Raju asked again.

The stranger smiled, a hint of mischief in their eyes.

"Someone who's been watching you, Raju. Someone who knows the truth."

And with that, they turned and disappeared into the shadows, leaving Raju with more questions than answers.

Raju's mind raced as he tried to process the documents. The stranger's words echoed in his mind: "It's just the tip of the iceberg."

He knew he had to dig deeper. But where to start?

Just then, his phone buzzed. A text from an unknown number:

"Meet me at the old warehouse at midnight. Come alone."

Raju's instincts screamed caution. But his curiosity got the better of him.

At midnight, he made his way to the warehouse, his heart pounding in his chest.

The stranger was already there, shrouded in shadows.

"You're taking a big risk trusting me," Raju said.

The stranger stepped forward, revealing a shocking identity:

It was Maria, the girl he had rescued from the trafficking ring.

"I've been working undercover," she said. "Gathering evidence to take down the corrupt officials."

Raju's eyes widened in shock. "You're the one who's been feeding me information?"

Maria nodded. "I knew I could trust you, Raju. Together, we can bring them down."

But as they spoke, Raju realized that Maria was hiding something.

What secrets was she keeping?

CHAPTER 17

The Hidden Agenda

Raju's eyes narrowed, sensing Maria's hesitation. "What are you not telling me?" he asked.

Maria's gaze faltered, and for a moment, Raju saw a glimmer of fear.

"I...I didn't want to put you in danger," she stammered.

Raju's grip on her arm tightened. "Tell me, Maria. What's going on?"

Maria took a deep breath, her voice barely above a whisper. "I've been working with someone on the inside. Someone who's been feeding me information, helping me gather evidence."

Raju's eyes widened. "Who?"

Maria hesitated, glancing around nervously. "I shouldn't have said that much. Please, Raju, you have to trust me."

Raju's mind raced. Who was Maria working with? And what was their true agenda?

Suddenly, a noise echoed through the warehouse, followed by footsteps.

Maria's eyes locked onto Raju's, a warning in their depths.

"It's them," she whispered. "We have to get out of here. Now."

Raju didn't hesitate. He grabbed Maria's hand, and together they fled into the night, pursued by unknown enemies.

CHAPTER 18

The Pursuit

Raju and Maria ran through the deserted streets, their footsteps echoing off the buildings. They didn't dare look back, fearing what they might see.

Finally, they reached Maria's car, parked in a nearby alley. They leapt in, and Maria sped away from the curb, tires screeching.

Raju glanced back, seeing a black SUV following them. "They're onto us," he shouted.

Maria floored it, weaving through traffic. Raju held on tight, his heart racing.

Suddenly, the SUV swerved, cutting them off. Maria slammed on the brakes, and Raju's heart skipped a beat.

The SUV's doors burst open, and men in suits poured out, surrounding them.

Raju and Maria were trapped.

But then, a motorcycle screeched to a halt beside them. The rider, a helmeted figure, gestured to Maria.
"Get on!" they yelled.

Maria didn't hesitate. She grabbed Raju's hand, and they leapt onto the motorcycle.

The rider sped away, leaving their pursuers in the dust.

As they caught their breath, Raju turned to Maria. "Who's our mysterious savior?"

Maria smiled, a hint of mischief in her eyes. "Someone who's been watching our backs."

Raju's eyes narrowed. "Who?"

Maria just smiled, and the motorcycle sped into the night.

CHAPTER 19

Back to the Streets

Raju's heart still raced from their narrow escape. The motorcycle rider had dropped them off at a safe house, but Raju knew he couldn't stay hidden forever.

He needed to get back to the streets, to find out who was behind the trafficking ring and take them down.

Maria tried to dissuade him, but Raju's mind was made up. He slipped out of the safe house, back into the night.

The familiar sights and sounds of the streets enveloped him, a mix of comfort and danger.

Raju made his way to the old clock tower, where he knew he'd find some of his old contacts.

As he climbed the stairs, a figure emerged from the shadows.

"Raju, I heard you were back," they said, a hint of a smile on their face.

Raju's eyes narrowed. "Who told you?"

The figure chuckled. "I have my ways. What brings you back to the streets?"

Raju's gaze locked onto theirs. "I'm looking for answers. Who's behind the trafficking ring?"

The figure hesitated, glancing around nervously. "I don't know if I should be telling you this..."

Raju's grip on their arm tightened. "Tell me."

The figure took a deep breath. "It's the Red Vipers. They're the ones running the show."

Raju's eyes widened. The Red Vipers were a notorious gang, known for their ruthlessness.

He knew he had to be careful. But he was ready for them.

CHAPTER 20

The Red Vipers

Raju's mind raced as he processed the information. The Red Vipers were a dangerous gang, and taking them down wouldn't be easy.

He spent the next few days gathering intel, talking to old contacts and gathering a team of trusted allies.

Finally, the night of the raid arrived. Raju and his team crept through the shadows, approaching the Red Vipers' hideout.

As they burst in, guns drawn, Raju's heart pounded in his chest. This was it.

The Red Vipers were caught off guard, but they quickly regrouped, putting up a fierce fight.

Raju's team fought bravely, but they were outnumbered. Just when it seemed like the tide was turning in favor of the Red Vipers, a mysterious figure appeared, taking down gang members with ease.

Raju's eyes widened as the figure revealed themselves - it was the motorcycle rider from earlier.

Together, they managed to subdue the Red Vipers and free the trafficking victims.

As the police arrived to take the gang members away, Raju turned to the mysterious figure.

"Who are you?" he asked, his voice filled with gratitude.

The figure smiled, pulling off their helmet to reveal a shocking identity - it was Ramesh's sister, Maya.

"I've been working undercover," she said. "Taking down the Red Vipers from the inside."

Raju's eyes widened in shock. He had so many questions.

But before he could ask any, Maya vanished into the night, leaving Raju stunned.

CHAPTER 21

The Aftermath

Raju's mind reeled as he processed the revelation. Maya, Ramesh's sister, had been working undercover to take down the Red Vipers.

He couldn't believe he had underestimated her. She was more than just a mysterious figure - she was a key player in the game.

As the police took the Red Vipers away, Raju knew that this was only the beginning. There were still more questions to answer, more secrets to uncover.

He turned to Maria, who had been watching the scene unfold. "We need to talk to Ramesh," he said. "Now."

Maria nodded, and together they made their way to Ramesh's hideout.

When they arrived, Ramesh was pacing back and forth, his eyes filled with worry. "Maya?" he asked, seeing the look on Raju's face.

Raju nodded. "She's the one who took down the Red Vipers. She's been working undercover."

Ramesh's eyes widened in shock. "I had no idea," he whispered.

Raju's grip on Ramesh's shoulder tightened. "We need to know more. What's going on, Ramesh?"

Ramesh took a deep breath, his eyes locked onto Raju's. "Maya and I...we've been working together. We've been trying to take down the trafficking ring from the inside."

Raju's eyes narrowed. "Why didn't you tell me?"

Ramesh's gaze faltered. "We didn't know who to trust. We couldn't risk it."

Raju's mind raced as he processed the information. There was still so much he didn't know.

But one thing was certain - he was in this now, deeper than ever before.

CHAPTER 22

The Hidden Truth

Raju's eyes locked onto Ramesh's, searching for any sign of deception. But all he saw was a deep-seated fear.

"What else are you hiding?" Raju asked, his voice firm but controlled.

Ramesh hesitated, glancing at Maria before answering. "There's something bigger at play here. Something that goes far beyond the trafficking ring."

Raju's grip on Ramesh's shoulder tightened. "What is it?"

Ramesh took a deep breath before speaking. "It's a conspiracy that reaches the highest levels of power. A conspiracy that involves corrupt officials, business leaders, and even law enforcement."

Raju's eyes widened in shock. He had suspected that there was more to the story, but he had never imagined anything like this.

Maria's voice was barely above a whisper. "What are we up against?"

Ramesh's gaze locked onto hers. "We're up against a powerful network that will stop at nothing to keep their secrets safe. We're talking about people who have the power to destroy lives with a single phone call."

Raju's mind reeled as he processed the information. He knew that they had to be careful, that one misstep could mean disaster.

But he also knew that they couldn't back down. Not now, not when they were so close to the truth.

CHAPTER 23

The Dark Alleys of Kolkata

Raju navigated the narrow streets of Kolkata, his eyes scanning the crowded alleys for any sign of danger. He had been walking for hours, trying to clear his head after the revelations about the conspiracy.

As he turned a corner, he stumbled upon a small tea stall, the aroma of brewing tea filling the air. He sat down on a rickety stool, ordering a cup of tea from the vendor.

As he sipped his tea, he noticed a figure watching him from across the alley. Tall, imposing, with piercing eyes that seemed to bore into Raju's soul.

Raju's instincts screamed warning, but he didn't flinch. He knew these streets, knew how to handle himself.

The figure began to walk towards him, its pace slow and deliberate. Raju's heart raced, his hand instinctively reaching for his pocket knife.

But as the figure approached, Raju saw something unexpected - a glimmer of recognition in its eyes.

"Raju?" the figure said, its voice low and gravelly. "Raju, is that you?"

Raju's eyes widened as he realized who it was - his old friend, Kunal, who had gone missing years ago.

"Kunal?" Raju said, his voice shaking with emotion. "Is that you?"

Kunal nodded, a hint of a smile on his face. "I've been watching you, Raju. I know what you're doing. And I'm here to help."

Raju's mind reeled as he tried to process this new development. What was Kunal doing here? And how did he know about the conspiracy?

CHAPTER 24

The Lost Friend

Raju's eyes locked onto Kunal's, searching for answers. "Where have you been?" he asked, his voice barely above a whisper.

Kunal's gaze faltered, and for a moment, Raju saw a glimmer of pain in his eyes. "I've been in hiding," he said. "I had to protect myself."

Raju's grip on Kunal's arm tightened. "From who?"

Kunal hesitated, glancing around nervously. "From the same people you're trying to take down. They've been hunting me for years."

Raju's mind raced as he processed the information. He had so many questions, but before he could ask any, Kunal continued.

"I've been gathering evidence, trying to build a case against them. But I need your help."

Raju nodded, determination coursing through his veins. "I'm in. What's the plan?"

Kunal smiled, a hint of mischief in his eyes. "We're going to take them down, Raju. Together."

As they spoke, Raju realized that Kunal's return was more than just a coincidence. It was a turning point in their fight against the conspiracy.

With Kunal by his side, Raju felt a sense of hope he hadn't felt in months. They could do this. They could take down the corrupt officials and bring justice to the streets of Kolkata.

But as they stood up to leave, Raju noticed something that made his heart skip a beat - a black SUV watching them from across the alley.

CHAPTER 25

The Watchers

Raju's eyes locked onto the black SUV, his heart racing with anticipation. Kunal followed his gaze, his expression grim.

"We've been made," Kunal whispered, his hand instinctively reaching for his phone.

Raju's grip on Kunal's arm tightened. "Don't," he warned. "We can't let them know we're onto them."
Kunal nodded, his eyes scanning the alley for an escape route.

But it was too late. The SUV's doors burst open, and men in suits poured out, surrounding them.

Raju's instincts kicked in, and he pushed Kunal behind him, ready to face their attackers.

But as he looked into the eyes of the men, he saw something that made his blood run cold - a hint of recognition.

They knew him. They had been waiting for him.

"Raju," one of the men sneered. "We've been expecting you."

Raju's mind raced as he tried to process the situation. Who were these men? And what did they want with him?

But before he could ask any questions, the men closed in, their movements swift and deadly.

Raju fought back with all his might, but he was outnumbered.

Just as all hope seemed lost, Kunal sprang into action, taking down their attackers with a skill that left Raju stunned.

But as they turned to run, Raju saw something that made his heart stop - Maria, being dragged away by the men in suits.

CHAPTER 26

The Disappearance

Raju's eyes widened in horror as he watched Maria being dragged away. He tried to rush after her, but Kunal held him back.

"Wait," Kunal whispered. "We can't save her if we get caught too."

Raju's mind raced as he watched the SUV speed away, Maria's screams echoing in his ears.

Who were these men? And what did they want with Maria?

Kunal pulled him into a nearby alley, his eyes scanning the rooftops.

"We need to be careful," Kunal said. "They could be watching us."

Raju nodded, his heart still racing with fear.

As they caught their breath, Raju realized that Kunal knew more than he was letting on.

"What do you know about Maria's disappearance?" Raju asked, his eyes narrowing.

Kunal hesitated, glancing around nervously.

"I didn't want to tell you," Kunal said. "But Maria was investigating something big. Something that could bring down the entire conspiracy."

Raju's eyes widened in shock.

"What was it?" he demanded.

Kunal leaned in close.

"Maria discovered a hidden server," Kunal whispered. "A server that contains all the evidence we need to take down the corrupt officials."

Raju's mind raced as he processed the information.

But before he could ask any more questions, Kunal's phone buzzed.

Kunal's eyes widened as he read the message.

"What is it?" Raju asked.

Kunal's face went white.

"It's a message from Maria," Kunal said. *"She's being held in an abandoned warehouse on the outskirts of town."*
Raju's heart skipped a beat.

"We have to go," Raju said. *"Now."*

CHAPTER 27

The City of Secrets

Raju's mind reeled as he tried to process Ramesh's betrayal. He had trusted him, considered him a friend.

But now, he was faced with a harsh reality - Ramesh was just another pawn in the conspiracy.

Determined to uncover the truth, Raju set out to explore Kolkata, to follow every lead, every hint.

He walked the streets, taking in the sights and sounds of the city. From the bustling markets of Burrabazar to the quiet alleys of Jorasanko, Raju searched for answers.

As he turned a corner, he stumbled upon a small, mysterious shop. The sign above the door read "Curios and Antiques".

Raju's instincts screamed warning, but he pushed open the door anyway.

Inside, the shop was dimly lit, the air thick with the scent of old books and dust.

A figure emerged from the shadows - an old man with piercing eyes.

"Welcome, Raju," the old man said. "I've been expecting you."

Raju's heart skipped a beat. "How do you know my name?"

The old man smiled. "I know many things, Raju. Things that could change the course of your life forever."

Raju's mind raced as he tried to process the old man's words.

"What do you know?" Raju asked, his voice barely above a whisper.

The old man leaned forward, his eyes glinting with mystery.

"I know the secrets of Kolkata," he said. "Secrets that have been hidden for centuries."

Raju's heart pounded with anticipation. He was one step closer to uncovering the truth.

The old man's words hung in the air like a challenge. Raju's curiosity was piqued, and he leaned forward, eager to hear more.

"Tell me," Raju said, his voice barely above a whisper.

The old man nodded, a small smile playing on his lips. "Kolkata has many secrets, Raju. Secrets that have been hidden for centuries. But I will share one with you."

Raju's eyes locked onto the old man's, his heart pounding with anticipation.

"The city is built on an ancient network of tunnels and passageways," the old man said. "Tunnels that stretch from the Hooghly River to the heart of the city."

Raju's mind raced as he tried to process the information. He had heard rumors of hidden tunnels, but he never thought they were real.

"Why are they hidden?" Raju asked.

The old man's expression turned serious. "They were built by the British, Raju. As an escape route, in case of an uprising. But they were also used for something more sinister."

Raju's eyes narrowed. "What do you mean?"

The old man leaned forward, his voice dropping to a whisper. "They were used to smuggle goods, Raju. And people."

Raju's heart skipped a beat as he realized the implications. The tunnels were still being used, still being hidden.

CHAPTER 28

The Tunnel Network

Raju's mind reeled as he tried to process the information. A network of hidden tunnels, used for smuggling and who knows what else.

The old man nodded, as if reading Raju's thoughts. "Yes, Raju. The tunnels are still used today. And I can show you where they are."

Raju's heart raced with excitement. He had to see this for himself.

The old man led him through the winding streets of Kolkata, pointing out hidden entrances and secret passages. Raju's eyes widened as he realized the extent of the network.

They finally arrived at a small, unassuming door in a quiet alley. The old man produced a key and unlocked the door, revealing a narrow stairway that descended into darkness.

"Follow me," the old man said, his voice barely above a whisper.

Raju hesitated for a moment, but his curiosity got the better of him. He followed the old man down the stairs, finding himself in a narrow, dimly lit tunnel.

The air was musty and dank, and Raju could hear the sound of dripping water echoing off the walls. He fumbled in his pocket for his phone, turning on the flashlight app to illuminate the tunnel.

As they walked, the tunnel began to slope downward, leading them deeper into the earth. Raju's heart pounded with excitement and fear.

Where were they going? And what would they find?

CHAPTER 29

The Hidden Chamber

The tunnel twisted and turned, leading them deeper into the earth. Raju's heart raced with anticipation, his mind racing with possibilities.

Finally, they arrived at a large stone door, adorned with ancient carvings. The old man produced a small key and unlocked the door, revealing a hidden chamber.

Raju's eyes widened as he stepped inside, his flashlight illuminating the room. The chamber was filled with ancient artifacts, treasures beyond his wildest dreams.

There were golden statues, precious jewels, and ancient texts, bound in leather and adorned with strange symbols.

Raju's mind reeled as he tried to take it all in. What was this place? And why was it hidden?

The old man smiled, as if reading Raju's thoughts. "This is the heart of Kolkata's secrets," he said. "A place where the city's true history is kept."

Raju's eyes landed on a small, leather-bound book. He picked it up, opening it to reveal pages filled with cryptic writing.

"What is this?" Raju asked, his voice barely above a whisper.

The old man's eyes gleamed with excitement. "That, Raju, is the diary of a British officer. A diary that reveals the truth about Kolkata's past."

Raju's heart skipped a beat as he began to read, the words revealing a story of conspiracy, deception, and hidden treasures. Chapter 33: The Truth Revealed

Raju's eyes scanned the pages, his mind racing with the implications. The diary revealed a shocking truth - the British had hidden a vast treasure in Kolkata, a treasure that had been lost for centuries.

But that was not all. The diary also revealed a dark secret - the treasure was cursed, and anyone who found it would be consumed by greed and destruction.

Raju felt a chill run down his spine as he read the final entry. He knew he had to find the treasure, but he also knew the risks.

Suddenly, he heard a noise behind him. He turned to see Ramesh, his eyes gleaming with greed.

"You'll never leave this place alive," Ramesh snarled, pulling out a gun.

Raju knew he had to act fast. He grabbed the diary and held it up, the pages fluttering in the wind.

"You'll never find the treasure without this," Raju said, a plan forming in his mind.

Ramesh snarled, pulling the trigger. But Raju was ready. He dodged the bullet and made a run for it, the diary clutched in his hand.

He navigated the tunnels, Ramesh hot on his heels. But Raju knew the tunnels like the back of his hand. He led Ramesh on a wild goose chase, finally losing him in the winding passages.

Finally, Raju emerged into the bright sunlight, the diary still clutched in his hand. He knew he had to destroy it, to prevent the treasure from falling into the wrong hands.

With a heavy heart, Raju burned the diary, the pages fluttering into ashes.

It was over. The secret was safe.

But as he turned to walk away, Raju felt a strange sensation. The curse, it seemed, was real.

CHAPTER 30

The Awakening

Raju felt the sensation of the curse spreading through his veins, consuming him. But as he looked down at his hands, he saw something strange - they were transparent, fading away like mist.

Suddenly, the world around him began to distort, like a reflection in rippling water. Raju's mind reeled as he realized the truth - he was dreaming.

With a start, Raju woke up, gasping for breath. He was in his small apartment, the morning sunlight streaming through the window.

It was all just a dream, he told himself. But as he looked around, he saw something that made his heart skip a beat - the diary, lying open on his table.

The pages were blank, except for a single sentence - "The truth is hidden in plain sight."

Raju's mind reeled as he realized the truth - the dream was real. The secrets of Kolkata, the treasure, the curse - it was all real.

But as he looked closer at the diary, he saw something else - a note, scribbled in the margin.

"Meet me at the old clock tower at midnight," it read. "Come alone."

Raju's heart pounded as he realized the truth - his adventure was far from over.

CHAPTER 31

The Midnight Meeting

Raju's mind raced as he wondered who could have written the note. He tried to brush it off as a prank, but the words lingered in his mind.

As the day wore on, Raju found himself glancing at the clock every few minutes. Midnight seemed to be approaching at a snail's pace.

Finally, the hour arrived. Raju made his way to the old clock tower, his heart pounding in his chest.

As he approached the tower, he saw a figure waiting in the shadows. It was Kunal, his friend from the beginning of the adventure.

"I see you got the message," Kunal said, a hint of a smile on his face.

Raju nodded, still trying to process what was happening.

"The dream was real," Kunal said, his voice low. "The secrets of Kolkata, the treasure, the curse - it's all real. And we're just getting started."

Raju's mind reeled as Kunal led him deeper into the night, the city unfolding before them like a labyrinth of secrets and lies.

And so, the adventure continued, into the heart of Kolkata's mysteries.

Epilogue

Raju stood on the banks of the Hooghly River, looking out at the city he had grown to love. It was a year since the events that had changed his life forever.

He thought back to the dream, the diary, and the midnight meeting. It had all been a journey, a journey to uncover the secrets of Kolkata.

But as he looked out at the city, he knew that there were still so many secrets hidden beneath its surface. Secrets waiting to be uncovered.

Raju smiled to himself, knowing that he would always be drawn to the unknown, to the mysteries that lay just beyond the edge of town.

And as he turned to walk away, he felt a strange sensation in his pocket. He reached in and pulled out a small piece of paper.

On it was a single sentence - "The next adventure begins now."

Raju's heart skipped a beat as he smiled, knowing that the journey was far from over.

Acknowledgements

I would like to express my deepest gratitude to the following individuals and influences that have shaped this novel:

To the city of Kolkata, whose vibrant streets, rich history, and resilient people inspired this story.

To my family, who supported me through countless hours of writing and rewriting.

To my friends, who offered valuable feedback, encouragement, and camaraderie.

To the literary giants who paved the way for this genre, your works have been a constant source of inspiration.

To the editors, proofreaders, and designers who helped refine this manuscript.

To the readers, who will bring this story to life with their imagination.

And to everyone who has walked the streets of Kolkata, carrying its secrets and stories within them.

Thank you.

Disclaimer

All characters, events, and locations depicted in this novel are entirely fictional and are not intended to be representative of real individuals, organizations, or places.

Any resemblance to actual persons, living or deceased, or to actual events or locations, is purely coincidental.

The author does not claim any connection or affiliation with any individual, organization, or entity mentioned in this work.

This novel is a work of fiction, intended for entertainment purposes only.

www.ingramcontent.com/pod-product-compliance
Lightning Source LLC
LaVergne TN
LVHW041623070526
838199LV00052B/3218